PUSHING THE LIMITS

A CHAPTER BOOK

BY MELISSA MCDANIEL

children's press®

A Division of Scholastic Inc.
New York Toronto London Auckland Sydney
Mexico City New Delhi Hong Kong
Danbury, Connecticut

ACKNOWLEDGMENTS

The author would like to thank all those who gave their time and knowledge to help with this book. In particular, special thanks go to the staff at the Iditarod Trail Committee; Michael Cohen; Kristie-Lee Ogilvie; and Naomi Flood.

Library of Congress Cataloging-in-Publication Data

McDaniel, Melissa.
Pushing the limits : a chapter book / by Melissa McDaniel.—1st ed.
  p. cm. — (True tales)
Includes bibliographical references and index.
ISBN 0-516-23734-9 (lib. bdg.)   0-516-24688-7 (pbk.)
1. Athletes—Biography—Juvenile literature. 2. Endurance sports—Juvenile literature.
I. Title. II. Series.
  GV697.A1M353 2004
  796'.092'2—dc22

2004005176

CONTENTS

Introduction   5

Chapter One
The Perfect Runner   6

Chapter Two
The Last Great Race   16

Chapter Three
Beyond the Limit   26

Chapter Four
The Strongest Woman in America   34

Glossary   44

Find Out More   46

Index   47

INTRODUCTION

All athletes push themselves. They want to go faster, higher, farther. Some people take this to the extreme.

Abebe Bikila ran barefoot through the dark streets. He raced 26 miles (42 kilometers) without stopping for a breath. Dick Mackey and his sled-dog team sped through more than 1,000 miles (1,609 kilometers) of frozen Alaskan wilderness, fighting the blinding snow and fierce wind. Julie Moss swam, biked, and ran for eleven hours. Then she crawled across the finish line, proving that through sheer will, the body can keep going, even after the muscles have given out. Still a teenager, Cheryl Haworth stepped up to a barbell and lifted more than 300 pounds (110 kilograms) into the air.

Each of these athletes pushed the limits. They pushed to see what they could do. They pushed to see what the human body is capable of. What they discovered is amazing.

CHAPTER ONE

THE PERFECT RUNNER

In 1960, the summer **Olympics** were held in Rome, Italy. Rome is sizzling hot in the summer. Because of the intense heat, the **marathon** was held at night. In the warm darkness, sixty-nine runners gathered for the beginning of the race. One of them, an **Ethiopian** (ee-thee-OH-pee-an) named Abebe Bikila, was in the very back of the group. Few people in the running world knew who Abebe was. He had run his first marathon only two months earlier.

Abebe Bikila

7

The starter's gun fired. The runners took off. Right away, the people lining the street noticed something unusual about Abebe. He wasn't wearing shoes. Abebe had always run barefoot. He was used to it. Before the Olympics, his trainer wanted to make sure that this was a good idea. He timed Abebe to see whether he ran faster with shoes or without. Sure enough, Abebe was faster without shoes.

As the marathon runners snaked their way through the streets of Rome, Abebe moved up in the crowd. He stayed just behind the leaders. Then, after about 12 miles (19 kilometers), Abebe shot into the lead. The only person who could keep up with him was a Moroccan named Rhadi ben Abdesselem.

The two men stayed even as they raced through the dark streets, their faces lit by the glow of torches.

Abebe had come a long way to race in Rome. He was born on August 7, 1932, in Jato, Ethiopia, in eastern Africa. He came from a large family. His father was a

shepherd and did not earn a lot of money. At age seventeen, Abebe joined the army. It seemed like a good way to make sure he had food and a place to sleep. Being in the army also gave Abebe the chance to run sometimes.

In 1959, he met a sports trainer from Sweden named Onni Niskanen. Niskanen could tell that Abebe had the makings of a great long-distance runner. Niskanen became Abebe's coach. Together, they worked to perfect Abebe's relaxed style of running. Soon, Abebe could run mile after mile without straining. Sometimes it seemed like he hardly broke a sweat.

Now, with less than a mile to go in the marathon, Abebe passed a huge monument called the Axum **Obelisk** (AH-buh-lisk). Axum was an ancient kingdom in the land that is now Ethiopia. Twenty years earlier, during World War II, Italian soldiers had stormed through Ethiopia. They had stolen the obelisk and carried it to Rome.

Axum Obelisk

Near the end of the marathon, Abebe breaks away from Rhadi ben Abdesselem.

As Abebe Bikila, the proud Ethiopian, passed the Axum Obelisk, he began his kick. He turned up the speed and pulled away from ben Abdesselem. By the time Abebe crossed the finish line, ben Abdesselem was trailing by 650 feet (200 meters).

Abebe had won the gold medal with a world record time of 2 hours, 15 minutes, 16 seconds. He had done far more than break the world record. He had shattered it. He had just run a marathon seven minutes faster than anyone had run a marathon before.

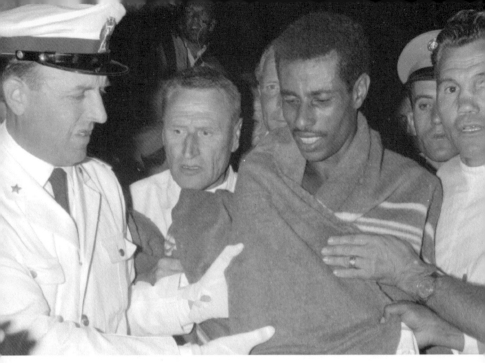

After the marathon, a tired Abebe is wrapped in a blanket.

He had done it in amazing style. He was calm, cool, and relaxed for 26 miles (42 kilometers). At the time, most marathon runners lost about 9 pounds (3.4 kilograms) in the course of a race. Most of this was from sweating. Abebe lost less than 1 pound (0.4 kilograms). He had shown the world that he was the perfect marathoner.

Abebe was the first black African to win an Olympic gold medal. He was no longer an unknown. Now he was famous around the world. He returned to Ethiopia a hero.

Four years later, the summer Olympics were held in Tokyo, Japan. This time, Abebe ran with shoes on. The shoes didn't seem to slow him down. Again he won the gold medal. Again he set a world record. No one had won two Olympic marathons before. His performance was all the more amazing because he had an operation to remove his **appendix** (uh-PEN-diks) only forty days earlier.

In 1968, Abebe went to Mexico City, Mexico, to try for a third gold medal. This time he would really push the limits of what a person can do. For 11 miles

Abebe accepts his gold medal after winning the marathon in the 1964 Summer Olympics.

(17 kilometers), he led the race. Finally, he could not go on. He had to drop out of the race. It turns out he had run the entire race with a broken foot.

That would be Abebe's last marathon. The following March he was in a terrible car crash. The crash left him **paralyzed** (PAR-uh-lyzd). He would never walk, or run, again. Four years later, on October 25, 1973, Abebe Bikila died. He was just forty-one years old.

Today, champions run the marathon in under 2 hours, 5 minutes. However, many people still think Abebe Bikila was the greatest marathoner of all time. He had turned his body into the perfect running machine. He had the will to always push himself to the limits.

Abebe raises his arms in victory after winning the 1964 Summer Olympics marathon in Tokyo.

CHAPTER TWO

THE LAST GREAT RACE

Dick Mackey and Rick Swenson stumbled down Front Street in Nome, Alaska. They took great, heaving breaths. Every time they breathed out, a puffy white cloud appeared, for it was cold. Each man was trying to control a team of dogs. The **Alaskan huskies** were pulling sleds piled with equipment.

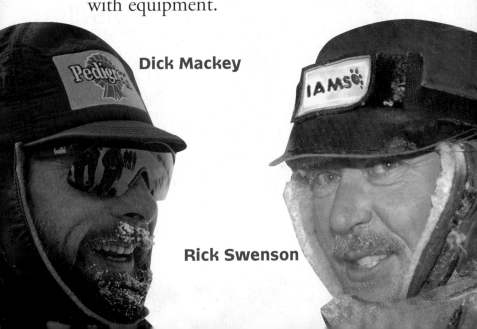

Dick Mackey

Rick Swenson

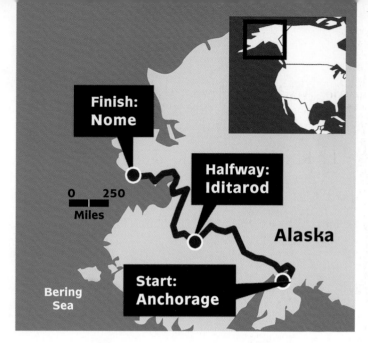

The route of the Iditarod

The men and their dogs had been racing for fourteen days. After all that time, it came down to this, a wild chase down Front Street. One team of dogs careened up on the sidewalk. The other became tangled up with a school bus. All around them people were cheering. They were watching the closest finish in the history of the **Iditarod** (eye-DIT-er-od) Trail Sled Dog Race.

People call the Iditarod "the Last Great Race." It is certainly one of the longest races in the world. It stretches over 1,000 miles (1,609 kilometers), from Anchorage to

Nome, Alaska. It winds through some of the world's most beautiful, and brutal, landscapes.

The Iditarod racers travel over rugged mountains and alongside frozen rivers. They thunder across the frozen **tundra** (TUN-druh) in temperatures far below zero. Brisk winds whip the heavy snow across their face so they can hardly see. After about ten days or so, the racers and their team of twelve to sixteen dogs come barreling into Nome, ready for a hero's welcome.

Although the actual miles vary, the official distance of the race is 1,049 miles (1,688 kilometers).   19

The Iditarod follows an old sled dog supply route. In the early twentieth century, cars couldn't make it through the winter storms in the mountains of Alaska. Railroad tracks had not been laid. Airplanes were not yet invented. So it was left to dogsled drivers, who are called "mushers," and their teams of dogs to bring mail and supplies to

Sled dogs pull heavy loads.

the Alaskan mining camps.

By the late 1920s, airplanes had taken over much of this work. Dogsleds were no longer the main way of getting around. Some people never forgot the hardy dogs and the

In the early 1900s, sled dogs were also used to pull lumber.

brave mushers. In 1973, the Iditarod Trail Sled Dog Race was started to honor them.

Five years later, Rick Swenson and Dick Mackey were racing toward the Iditarod finish line. Dick wasn't from Alaska. He had grown up in New Hampshire. In 1959, the year Alaska became a state, Dick had just lost his job. Like many people, he thought of Alaska as a wild, faraway place where a person could start over. So Dick headed off to find a new life.

His first winter in Alaska, Dick saw a sled dog race in Anchorage. It looked like fun, and Dick soon found himself with a puppy. By the following winter he had six dogs. He was hooked.

At the 1977 Iditarod, Dick had come in sixth. He very much wanted to win in 1978. He and his dogs trained hard for months. Dick was ready when he arrived in Anchorage for the start of the race.

Dick decided that he would let Rick Swenson lead most of the way. This forced Rick to break the trail. Rick's dogs had to plow through the fresh snow. Then, at night, when Rick stopped to make camp, Dick would pass him. He would go just a little bit farther.

Dick Mackey races to the finish line.

When they set off each morning, Rick would again take the lead. Dick would be right behind him. For the last 800 miles (1,300 kilometers) of the race, Dick and Rick were never more than 100 yards (91 meters) apart. They stayed together all through the thick forests and the driving snow.

Coming into Nome, Rick and Dick were neck and neck. At the end, both men ended up off their sleds, madly dashing down Front Street. Their dogs were racing ahead of them. Dick watched his lead dogs, Skipper and Shrew, cross the finish line. Then he **collapsed**

A sign for the Iditarod Trail Race

in the snow. He couldn't believe it. After
two weeks on the trail, it was a photo finish.

Other Iditarods also burn brightly in
the memory of Alaskans. In 1985, Libby
Riddles became the first woman to win the
race. In 2002, Martin Buser became the first
musher to finish the race in less than nine
days. However, everyone still talks about the
1978 Iditarod, when Dick Mackey beat
Rick Swenson by just one second.

CHAPTER THREE

BEYOND THE LIMIT

One warm February day in 1982, a young woman slowly ran down a street in Kona, Hawai'i. Sweat streamed from her head. Her eyes were dull and unfocused. The woman weaved a bit, and then she stumbled. She fell to the ground. She lay there a moment. Then she slowly pushed herself up with her arms. She struggled to her feet.

Julie Moss

With every bit of **determination** left in her **exhausted** body, she forced her feet to move. She was again running, but very slowly.

The woman's name is Julie Moss. That day in 1982, she was competing in her first **Ironman triathlon**. The Ironman is the ultimate **endurance** sport. No other sport pushes athletes as far and as hard as the Ironman. In an Ironman triathlon, the racers must first swim 2.4 miles (3.8 kilometers) in the ocean. Then they ride

The Ironman triathlon is made up of three parts.

Swimming

bicycles for another 112 miles (180 kilometers). Then, finally, they run a full marathon. That's 26 miles (42 kilometers) of pounding the pavement. The event is so **grueling** (GROO-uh-ling) that people say just finishing an Ironman is a victory.

Julie Moss was never much of an athlete. She had played sports in high school, but she wasn't very competitive. "I used to dread getting called onto the court for volleyball, or having to serve in tennis," she says.

Bicycling

Marathon running

By 1982, she was twenty-three years old and in college. She was studying the effect of exercise on the body. Doing the triathlon was part of her research.

Julie Moss didn't expect to win the Ironman. She just wanted to finish. She wanted to learn how such a long and hard race would affect her body.

During the race she learned something else about herself. She found out that she cared about winning. By the time she was done with the swim and the bike ride, she had a big **lead**. Now she cared. Now Julie wanted to win. She began pushing herself to keep going, as fast as she possibly could.

With about 5 miles (8 kilometers) to go, Julie's legs became wobbly and she fell for the first time. She got up and kept running. Again she fell. Again she got back on her feet. She fell and got up a few more times. With about 20 yards (18 meters) to the finish line, Julie Moss fell one last time. This time she couldn't get up, so she began to crawl.

The Ironman triathlon was being shown on a television program called *ABC's Wide World of Sports*. All over the country people watched in amazement as Julie Moss crawled toward the finish line. They couldn't believe her grit and determination. She just refused to give up. People phoned their friends and told them to turn on their television sets and watch.

Julie crawls her way to the finish line.

Julie inched toward the finish line. Just before she reached it, a racer named Kathleen McCartney passed her. Despite her heroic effort, Julie had come in second.

That didn't matter. Julie Moss was the story of the day. Jim McKay, the longtime host of *Wide World of Sports*, called it the most **inspiring** moment he had ever seen in sports.

Thousands of people who saw Moss crawl toward the finish line that day decided to try the Ironman. Julie's amazing performance helped make the Ironman triathlon a popular event.

It took Julie eleven hours to finish the Ironman. Today's champions complete the event in less than nine hours. However, Julie remains the ultimate **symbol** (SIM-bul) of the Ironman. Because on that day in 1982, she pushed herself to the limit, and beyond.

ie continues to push herself to the limits. In 2003, she
mpeted in the Ironman triathlon for the seventh time.

CHAPTER FOUR

THE STRONGEST WOMAN IN AMERICA

Cheryl Haworth is big. She weighs nearly 300 pounds (110 kilograms). Cheryl Haworth is also strong. She can walk up to a 300-pound (110-kilogram) barbell and heave it above her head. Cheryl is the strongest woman in America.

Cheryl Haworth

Cheryl competes at the Goodwill Games in 2001.

Cheryl at five years old

Even as a child, Cheryl was strong. She grew up in Savannah, Georgia, on a large piece of land that was filled with trees. When she was eleven years old, she and the boys who lived nearby would cut down trees and build huge tree houses. It was Cheryl who would carry the big logs.

When Cheryl was young, she loved softball. She had a great arm and could really hit. When she was thirteen years old, her softball coach suggested she do some weight training at a local gym so she would be in better shape for the next season.

Cheryl was lucky. The gym in Savannah happened to be the best place for weightlifting training in the country, for both men and women. The first day Cheryl walked into the gym, a coach named Sheryl Cohen began working with her. After a few minutes, Sheryl went looking for her husband, Michael, who ran the gym. "Michael," she said, "this Haworth is the fastest, strongest girl I've ever seen."

Michael Cohen became Cheryl's coach.

Cheryl became a very good weightlifter very quickly. Seven months after the day she walked into that gym, she won her first junior national title. By the time she was sixteen years old, she was the national champion for people of any age. She now holds every United States weightlifting record for her weight class.

Cheryl competing in the Senior Nationals in 1999

Weightlifting takes great **dedication**. Cheryl gets up at 6 A.M. and goes to school. After school, she works out at the gym for three hours. It's very tiring. "I know I have to work hard to get what I want, which is to stay one of the top women in the world," says Cheryl.

"You can't give yourself time to think, 'Oh, I don't want to do this today. I'm too tired.'" She knows that to be the best, she has to keep pushing, always pushing.

Many people think that because Cheryl is so big, she must be out of shape. "It's a **stereotype** I've learned to ignore," she says. In fact, Cheryl is in great shape. Sure, she's big, but her thighs are as hard as a rock. Weightlifting is about more than just strength. To be a great weightlifter, you also have to be very flexible and very fast. Cheryl can do a full **split**. She can jump 33 inches (84 centimeters) into the air.

Weightlifting has always been a man's sport. Women, even women athletes, weren't supposed to be too strong. Over the years, though, more and more women began lifting weights to get in shape. Some of them were thrilled with the challenge. They began to push themselves. Just how much could they lift? In 2000, women's weightlifting finally became an Olympic sport.

Cheryl was just seventeen years old when she went to Sydney, Australia, for the 2000 Olympic Games. She was under a lot of pressure. Everyone expected her to win a medal. Cheryl is tough. She could handle the pressure. She had to deal with a lot besides that.

Many reporters couldn't get past her size. They thought that because she is large, she must be unhappy. Cheryl doesn't worry about what people think of her. Her friend Cara Heads-Lane, who is also a weightlifter, says that Cheryl "doesn't worry about what this little boy or that little boy might be thinking about her." Instead, she just focuses on what she needs to do.

Cheryl competing in the 2000 Summer Olympics

At the Olympics, she did just that. Cheryl faced much more experienced weightlifters, but she still managed to come in third. Cheryl was thrilled with her bronze medal. She considers the Olympics the high point of her life.

Most weightlifters reach their peak at around age thirty. That means that Cheryl has a lot of years to keep getting stronger and faster and better. She's already the strongest woman in America. Maybe one day, she'll prove to be the strongest woman in the world. To do that, though, she'll have to outlift such powerhouses as Ding Meiyuan of China and Agata Wrobel of Poland.

Cheryl thinks she can do just that. "I do feel I can keep going and **accomplish** my goals," she says. "That's the message I want to get out, especially to girls: You can do anything."

Cheryl celebrates winning the bronze medal at the 2000 Summer Olympics.

GLOSSARY

accomplish to finish something successfully

Alaskan husky a strong dog with a thick coat used to pull sleds

appendix (uh-PEN-diks) a small tube inside the body that leads to the large intestine

collapse to fall down or cave in

dedication the act of working hard for a set purpose

determination being firm in purpose

endurance the ability to put up with something for a long time

Ethiopian (ee-thee-OH-pee-an) a person who comes from Ethiopia, a country in Africa

exhausted very tired

grueling (GROO-uh-ling) very demanding and tiring

Iditarod (eye-DIT-er-od) a yearly dogsled race that starts in Anchorage, Alaska, and ends in Nome, Alaska

inspire to fill with excitement

Ironman triathlon a competition featuring a swimming race, a bicycling race, and a marathon

lead the front position in a race

marathon a race that covers a distance of 26 miles (42 kilometers) and 385 yards (352 meters)

obelisk (AH-buh-lisk) a tall column that ends in a triangular shape

Olympics a competition held every four years for athletes from all over the world

paralyzed (PAR-uh-lyzd) to have lost feeling or movement in the arms and legs

split a move in which a person's legs are spread in opposite directions

stereotype an opinion or belief that is not based on fact

symbol (SIM-bul) an object or person who stands for something else

tundra (TUN-druh) the frozen, treeless land of the coldest parts of the world

FIND OUT MORE

The Perfect Runner
www.terra.com/specials/sportsicons/bikila_en.html
Read more about Abebe Bikila's great career.

The Last Great Race
www.iditarod.com
This site tells you all about the Iditarod.

Beyond the Limit
http://vnews.ironmanlive.com/vnews/topstories/1055951669/
Read what Julie Moss has to say about her first, stunning
Ironman.

The Strongest Woman in America
www.usoc.org/cfdocs/athlete_bios/bio_template.cfm?ID=295
&Sport=Weightlifting
Read a short biography of Cheryl Haworth.

More Books to Read

The Iditarod: Story of the Last Great Race by Ian Young,
Capstone Press, 2003

The Ironman Triathlon by Bill Scheppler, Rosen Publishing
Group, 2002

Summer Olympics by Clive Gifford, Houghton Mifflin, 2004

Weightlifting by Bob Knotts, Children's Press, 2000

INDEX

ABC's Wide World of Sports, 31
Alaska, 20, 21, 22
Alaskan huskies, 16, 17
Anchorage, Alaska, 18, 22
Axum Obelisk, 10, 11
ben Abdesselem, Rhadi, 8, 11
Bikila, Abebe, 4, 5, 6-15
Buser, Martin, 24
Cohen, Michael, 37
Cohen, Sheryl, 37
Ethiopia, 9, 10, 12
Goodwill Games, 35
Haworth, Cheryl, 4, 5, 34-43
Heads-Lane, Cara, 41
Iditarod Trail Race, 18-22, 24
Ironman triathlon, 28-33
Jato, Ethiopia, 9
Kona, Hawai'i, 26
Mackey, Dick, 4, 5, 16, 21-24

marathons, 6, 11-12, 13, 14, 15, 29
McCartney, Kathleen, 32
McKay, Jim, 32
Meiyuan, Ding, 42
Mexico City, Mexico, 13
Moss, Julie, 4, 5, 26-33
New Hampshire, 21
Niskanen, Onni, 10
Nome, Alaska, 16, 18, 19, 23, 24
Olympic Games, 6, 13, 15, 40-43
Riddles, Libby, 24
Rome, Italy, 6, 8, 9, 10
Savannah, Georgia, 36, 37
Senior Nationals, 38
Swenson, Rick, 16, 21-24
Sydney, Australia, 40
Tokyo, Japan, 13
Wrobel, Agata, 42

PHOTO CREDITS

MEET THE AUTHOR

 Melissa McDaniel is a children's book editor and author. She has written nearly twenty books for young people. Melissa has written on subjects ranging from movies to science. She particularly enjoys writing and learning about people with amazing stories to tell.

Although Melissa has never run a marathon, she does spend endless hours chasing around after her daughter, Iris. Melissa and her family live in New York City.